Spellbound Ponies

Dancing and Dreams

STACY GREGG

HarperCollins *Children's Books*

First published in Great Britain by
HarperCollins *Children's Books* in 2021
HarperCollins *Children's Books* is a division of HarperCollins*Publishers* Ltd
HarperCollins Publishers
1 London Bridge Street
London SE1 9GF

www.harpercollins.co.uk

HarperCollins*Publishers*
1st Floor, Watermarque Building, Ringsend Road
Dublin 4, Ireland
1

ISBN 978-0-00-840302-7

Typeset in Cambria 12pt/24pt

Printed and bound in the UK using 100% renewable electricity at CPI Group
(UK) Ltd

MIX
Paper from
responsible sources
FSC™ C007454

This book is produced from independently certified FSC™ paper
to ensure responsible forest management.

For more information visit: www.harpercollins.co.uk/green

For Harper, Pippa and Breslin

Chapter One

In the haunted gloom of Pemberley Stables, magical things were afoot. A strange glow could be seen coming from the door of the last stall in the row. The brass name plaque on that door was beginning to shimmer in a mystical way.

It would all have been very mysterious for nine-year-old Olivia Campbell – if she hadn't seen it happen so many times before. This was Olivia's sixth

Spellbound Pony summoning so she knew the ropes!

'All the same, it's very sudden, isn't it?' Olivia said to her best friend, Eliza. 'I mean, we've only just finished saving the last one. Dear sweet Grumpy Gus – he was a real challenge too. And now look – the plaque is glowing; soon a name will appear and when we step over that threshold a new pony will be with us once more. I wonder what kind of enchantment the Pemberley Witch has cast this time?'

'It will be something diabolically different, I expect,' Eliza replied. 'The witch is very tricky, always cursing each pony in their own way.'

'Well, I'm not afraid,' Olivia said. 'Every time so far we've beaten her dark magic and rescued the ponies.'

There was a whinny from the other end of the corridor and Olivia cast her eyes down the row of stalls to see that the Pemberley ponies all had their heads out over the doors to watch what was going on.

Olivia bounded forward to stroke the muzzle of the beautiful black mare in the first stall. 'My darling Bess, you were a highway horse living a life of crime before we convinced you to change your ways.'

Eliza stepped up to feed an apple to the next pony, a dashing dapple-grey. 'And you, handsome Prince, were greedy and far too fond of cakes.'

The white mare in the next stall nickered for attention and Olivia put a braid in her forelock. 'Sparkle, you are so gorgey-porgey! It's hard to believe you were once messy and determined to stay a mud heap.'

'Or that Champ was a terrible fibber,' Eliza added, 'or that Gus was a dreadful grumpy guts. And now all five of them are unbound from the witch's spell that kept them trapped in time and they're real-life ponies again.'

'Which brings us,' Olivia said, 'to the final stall in the stables. Can you believe we've reached the last one, Eliza? If we can find the true nature of the pony's curse and break the spell, then we've done it!'

'Two brave girls together,' Eliza said, 'just like the witch's spell says.'

That spell was carved in stone on the ivy-clad wall outside the front door of Pemberley Stables and Olivia knew it off by heart.

The deepest magic binds these stables
Unless two brave girls can turn the tables.
The curse on each horse must be found,
Then break their spell to be unbound.

'For two hundred years the witch's spell kept them stuck, each one doomed in their own way,' Eliza marvelled. 'And for two hundred years I've remained at the stables to take care of the ponies. Before you came I tried so many times to free them, but I could never do it alone.'

Once Olivia had arrived, however, she and Eliza had become best friends and together the girls had succeeded again and again against the witch's powerful magic.

'And now we've reached the final stall,' Olivia said solemnly.

'Are you ready?' Eliza asked. 'You know all you have to do is say the name and walk over the threshold and the Spellbound Pony will appear.'

Olivia stood at the door and stared at the name that had appeared in glowing, magical letters.

'Oh!' She hesitated. 'I can't say it!'

MARGOT

'What do you mean? You absolutely must!' Eliza insisted. 'Please, Olivia – it's the only way to save the pony.'

'No, no,' Olivia laughed. 'I don't mean I won't do it – I mean I can't. I don't know how to pronounce the name, you see. It's quite a tricky word!'

The name on the plaque read: MARGOT.

Eliza giggled. 'Oh, I see! It is quite a unique name, I suppose, although it was very common two hundred and nine years ago when I was born. It's the name of Mama's prized dancing-dressage mare, and the thing to know about Margot is that her "T" is silent.'

'Gotcha,' said Olivia, promptly stepping over the threshold and saying out loud, 'MAR-GO!'

Almost instantly, the stall began to fill with mystical mist. It rose up in a spooky way from the straw on the stable floor, creeping up Olivia and Eliza's ankles, then reaching their knees, until very soon the entire space was full of an enchanted haze and Olivia couldn't see a thing.

'Here we go . . .' she whispered. 'Any moment now, Margot will arrive and— Hang on – what's all that thumping about?'

'I can hear something crashing!' Eliza squeaked. There was another bang and thud as the floor beneath them began to shudder and lurch.

'It feels like dinosaur-stomping,' Eliza suggested.

'Or perhaps a hippopotamus bouncing up and down on a Swiss ball?' Olivia added.

There was even more banging and thumping, and suddenly the most enormous CRASH! And then the mist cleared and a pony was lying in front of Olivia and Eliza in a heap on the straw.

'Ooffff!' The pony sat up, looking dazed, and Olivia could see that she was a very pretty dapple-grey with sparkling dark eyes. 'Doozy-dazy! Where am I?'

'You're in your stall at Pemberley Stables.' Olivia said. 'You must be Margot. I'm Olivia and this is Eliza. We just summoned you.'

'Did you really?' The grey mare looked up with wide eyes and batted her long lashes at Olivia. 'Oh, I'm so embarrassed about all of this. I mean, I'm not very good at making entrances at the best of times. Now here I go like a complete clot, as usual, stumbling in! I must have tripped over my own hooves and the next thing I knew, I was falling, down, down, down . . . and now here I am!'

'Stumbling in?' Olivia asked as she watched the grey pony struggling to her feet.

'Oh, this straw is more slippery than it looks!' Margot muttered as she wobbled about. 'Uh-oh. Oh no – got my fetlocks in a tangle again. Down I go!'

'Crikey!' Olivia hurried over to the pony, who was now in a heap on the straw once more. 'Are you all right?'

'Oh, quite,' Margot said. 'I can't imagine what went wrong there. I must admit I was a bit overwhelmed, what with meeting new people, and the next minute I was on the floor!'

'Perhaps just lie there for a bit?' Eliza suggested. 'Until you find your feet?'

'Aha! Eliza, I think her feet are the problem,' Olivia said. 'Poor Margot – the curse has given her two left feet!'

'Well, for a pony that would be quite normal,' Eliza pointed out. 'All ponies have two left feet.'

Olivia rolled her eyes. 'All right, then. I mean, four . . . Margot has four left feet.'

'Oh, I see,' Eliza said. 'Margot has been cursed to be clumsy!'

Chapter Two

Margot looked up at the girls through her long lashes. 'Really?' she said softly. 'Me? Clumsy? I mean, I'm not one to argue. In fact, I never argue with anyone and rarely say boo to a goose. I never like to give an opinion – I hardly dare speak up. All the same – me, clumsy? It can't possibly be true!'

'And why is that, Margot?' Olivia asked.

Margot bit her lip and looked down at her hooves for a long time as if she didn't want to speak, but then at last she blurted out, 'Because I love to dance! I want to be a famous dancer, in fact. And I can't be a dance-sensation if I'm cursed to be a clumsy clot!'

'Oh, poor, poor pony!' Eliza looked like she might cry. 'That witch really is a wretch! Imagine cursing Margot to be clumsy.'

'We will help you, Margot, I promise,' Olivia said. 'Let's begin by getting you on your feet again.' She took hold of Margot's halter and tried to pull her up but the grey pony managed to slip loose of her halter entirely so that Olivia fell back and banged into the water trough.

'Owww!'

'Gosh, you're quite clumsy too, aren't you?' Eliza pointed out.

'The halter slipped,' Olivia groaned.

'Are you all right?' Eliza asked.

'I'm fine.' Olivia rubbed her sore elbow. 'I whacked myself on the water trough. It's quite cramped in here . . .'

'That's it!' Eliza exclaimed. 'This stall is hardly helping matters. It's very small. We need somewhere bigger so that Margot can dance properly and get in some practice.'

'I suppose that might help,' Olivia agreed, 'but where could we go?'

'Ohhh!' Eliza's brilliant green eyes blazed brightly. 'I know just the place. It's a very grand ballroom – I danced there myself back in the day!'

'A grand ballroom?' Margot looked very worried. 'Will there be lots of people there? I'm not very good with lots of people. All those introductions and having to say hello. Besides, ummm, I have nothing to wear!'

'Yes, you do!' Eliza pointed to the rack of ballet tutus at the back of the stall.

'Where did that clothing rack appear from?' Margot wondered out loud as Olivia bounded over to look through the clothes.

'Ohhhh, the cherry-red tutu!' Eliza squeaked with delight. 'Pull that one out, Livvy! It would look gorgeous on a grey pony!'

'It's a bit bright, isn't it?' Margot said. 'I don't really like to draw attention to myself. I usually like to wear colours that make me blend into the walls.'

'Oh, surely not!' Eliza giggled. 'Silly pony! You'll look lovely in this. Let's put it on now.'

Olivia helped the pony into her tutu.

'It looks very good on you, Margot,' Olivia said.

Margot blushed. 'I'm not used to so much attention,' she said softly. 'I'm very shy and—'

'Look!' Eliza pointed to the straw on the floor
of the stall. 'Enchanted mist! This is it – we're on
our way!'

'On our way where, exactly?' Olivia asked. 'Eliza,
you never explained where it is that we are going . . .'

At that moment, the mist cleared and they were no longer in the musty old stall in the stables. They had been whisked away and now found themselves in a very grand, sparkly ballroom, hung with crystal

chandeliers and strung with twinkling lights and
fresh-scented garlands of gardenias.

'Gosh, look at the wonderful decorations!' Eliza
said. 'It must be a special occasion. I've never seen
the ballroom like this before.'

'You've been here before?' Olivia asked.

'Well, of course I have!' Eliza replied. 'This is the ballroom at Mama's house.'

'Your mama's house?' Olivia felt a chill run down her spine. 'Do you mean to say you've taken us back to your old home?'

'That's right,' Eliza said. 'We're in the ballroom at Pemberley Manor.'

'But, Eliza,' Olivia shrieked, 'your mother is super-scary! She's the one who had the ponies cursed in the first place!'

'Oh, she didn't mean to do that, really,' Eliza said. 'I'm quite certain she feels sorry about it now. She was just upset at the time, that's all. I mean it was a terribly sudden chain of events. When she let me ride out on the hunt field that day on my pony Chessie, I did promise her I would stay at the back. But Chessie became too strong for me and before you knew it, we had overtaken Horace the Hunt Master. It was all going swimmingly until Chessie stuck his leg down that rabbit hole. After the accident, Mama was desperately sad about my death, so that was when she paid the Pemberley Witch the six gold coins to curse all the ponies in the stables. It was a broken heart that made her do it. She missed me and she still does. All she ever wanted was for me to come home again . . .'

'That's right,' a spooky voice agreed. Eliza and Olivia turned to see Lady Luella hovering in a ghostly fashion in the doorway. She looked very beautiful with her russet hair tumbling over her shoulders in thick waves, and her scarlet lips and alabaster skin. Her dark eyebrows were raised in an imperious arch above her equally dark eyes.

'All I ever wanted was for Eliza to come home,' Lady Luella repeated, 'and now, my dear heart, my daughter, my dreams have come true. You've come back to me at last.'

Chapter Three

Eliza's green eyes misted with sorrow. 'Ohhh, Mama, I haven't come home to stay,' she admitted. 'I'm only here to use the ballroom for dancing practice.'

A flicker of disappointment passed over Lady Luella's face, but she quickly recovered her composure. 'Of course. Well, I'm glad you're still practising your dancing, at least, Eliza. You were always a lovely ballerina.'

'Oh no, Mama,' Eliza said, 'it's not me that's practising – it's Margot!'

'Where is Margot, anyway?' Olivia wondered aloud.

'Ahem. Over here,' Margot's voice called.

'I can't see her,' Eliza said. 'Do you think she's turned invisible? Or perhaps disappeared completely?'

'No,' a tiny voice said from the other end of the room. 'I'm here.'

'Where exactly is here?' Lady Luella enquired. 'Come on, Margot, show yourself!'

'Gosh,' Eliza said as Margot emerged meekly from behind a pillar in the shadows at the rear of the room. 'I've never seen a pony who was able to hide like that before.'

'You'd hardly know she was there!' Olivia agreed.

'Come on, Margot!' Lady Luella said. 'On the trot!

Get over here – I'm starting to lose patience. Hurry up!' She turned to Olivia. 'What's wrong with this one, then? Grumpy?'

'No,' Olivia said, 'that was Gus. We solved that one.'

Lady Luella glared at Margot. 'Perhaps she's a naughty thieving sort, then? Rather sneaky, hiding in the shadows like that.'

'No, Mama,' Eliza said, 'that was Bess who liked to steal things, remember?'

'So what, precisely, is this pony cursed with?' Lady Luella asked.

At that moment Margot appeared in front of Lady Luella, shaking like a leaf. 'Ohhhh.' The dapple-grey mare trembled. 'Ohhhhhh!'

'This is very strange indeed! Doesn't she speak?' Lady Luella stared at the dumbstruck pony before her. 'I thought the whole point of these Spellbound Ponies was that they were a bunch of chatterboxes and it was virtually impossible to shut them up?'

'Now that you mention it,' Olivia said, 'Margot is frightfully, awfully quiet for a Spellbound Pony.'

Lady Luella glared down at the pony. 'What, exactly, is wrong with you?' she demanded.

'Ohhhh, my . . . Your Ladyship,' Margot said softly as she bowed her head and dropped down on one knee, 'Livvy and Eliza, the girls, tell me that I'm clumsy.'

Seeing that Margot wasn't going to add anything further, Olivia leaped in. 'It seems that this time the Pemberley Witch's curse has given her four left feet.'

'That truly is a terrible curse to be a clumsy clot.' Lady Luella shook her head. 'Come on, then. Arise, pony – let's get a better look at you!'

Lady Luella looked long and hard at Margot. 'Why, it's Margot! You were once my prize dressage mare with such fabulous dance moves! Always so beautiful with those lovely grey dapples and that silken mane.'

Margot blushed. 'Thank you, Your Ladyship,' she managed to blurt out before falling silent again and gazing very intently at her hooves, her cheeks burning like hot coals from being the centre of attention.

'Margot still loves to dance, don't you, Margot?' Eliza said, speaking up for the pony. 'We were hoping we could use the ballroom so that she had some space to practise. The stall at the stables is far too small.'

'To get her groove back, you see, and become less clumsy,' Olivia explained. 'We need somewhere where she won't bang into things – or into us!'

'Impossible, I'm afraid.' Lady Luella shook her head. 'The grand ballroom is fully booked today.'

'Booked?' Eliza said. 'Who could possibly have booked the ballroom?'

As Eliza asked the question, the sound of music suddenly filled the room and a woman with a bushy halo of violet hair, beady eyes and an enormous warty nose swept in through the doors of the ballroom. She was dressed in a very pouffy black sequined ballet tutu and on her feet she wore high-heeled red glittery shoes.

'La la la! I'm a dancing queen!' the woman shrieked as she threw herself into the splits and sprawled across the ballroom floor.

'*Cha-cha ca-chooo*, I'm coming through!' A rotund figure came running out to join her on the dance floor. He was dressed in a sparkling candy-striped leotard and he made a spectacular slide on one knee to do the splits and then bounce back up again.

'Hang on a minute!' Olivia boggled. 'That dancer is Horace the Hunt Master! I hardly recognised him without his hunting boots and riding jacket!'

'It really is Horace!' Eliza exclaimed. 'I wouldn't have believed it but you can tell by the way his head is bobbling about.'

When Eliza and her pony Chessie had cut Horace off on the hunting field that fateful day and caused him to fall from his mount, the hunt master had broken his neck.

'Two hundred years later and his head is still wobbly,' Eliza observed, 'especially when he's boinging about like that!'

'Horace! You and me! It takes two to tango!' the woman in the black tutu shrieked. Swooping like a spangled crow, she snatched Horace by the hand and propelled him across the dance floor with her cheek pressed up against his ruddy face.

'One-two-three-dip!' Horace danced her backwards and clutched her in an embrace that would have been quite elegant, except that her warty nose was so long it got stuck in the crook of his wobbly neck and they both collapsed in a heap on the floor.

'Never mind, Pembers!' Horace bounced back to his feet. 'Let's keep our distance this time and throw some shapes!'

'Good idea!' His dance partner picked herself up and began to wiggle and wave her arms. 'Look at me! I'm jiving!'

'And I'm doing a paso doble!' Horace strutted

super-quickly across the dance floor.

'Look at his little legs go!' Eliza said.

'He's certainly on form,' Lady Luella had to agree. 'If those two can perform like that in the dance-off, then they might win the contest.'

'Contest?' Eliza said. 'What contest?'

'My dear daughter,' Lady Luella replied, 'I'm having a dance contest right here at the manor. I thought you knew? In fact, I assumed you must have entered Margot. After all, if she were to win, it would prove absolutely that she isn't clumsy.'

'What a brilliant idea!' Eliza said. 'Oh, Livvy, did you hear that? We simply have to enter. I'm certain that if Margot wins, it will break the spell.'

'Hah! You'll never win!'

It was Horace. He had danced his way across the room and was now tangoing right in front of them

with the warty-nosed woman. Together, pressed
cheek to cheek, they made a dramatic dive and
Horace dropped to one knee and held his dancing
partner above his head.

'Grand finale move! *Ta-dah!*' Horace chortled as they both took a bow. The woman in the black tutu cackled and gave Horace's hand a victorious slap.

'High five, my floppy-necked friend!' she squawked. 'You two girls are going to be sorry losers! We're bound to beat you! The contest is in the bag.'

'Who is his dance partner, anyway?' Olivia asked. 'She seems extremely nasty.'

'Oh,' Eliza said, 'she's nasty all right. Nastier than you can possibly imagine, Livvy. It's thanks to her dark magic that the ponies have been trapped in time for two hundred years!'

'You don't mean . . .' Olivia gasped.

'I do!' Eliza said. 'Horace's dance partner is none other than the Pemberley Witch!'

Chapter Four

Back at Pemberley Stables, Olivia and Eliza called a
meeting with Margot.

'We're really in trouble now,' Olivia admitted. 'It's
clear that Horace and the Pemberley Witch are in
cahoots.'

'What's a car-hoot?' Eliza asked.

'Cahoots! It means they're working together,'
Olivia explained. 'They're trying to stop Margot

winning the dance contest so the spell will remain unbroken!'

'Oh, boo-hoo!' Margot suddenly broke out into dramatic sobs. 'What a meanie that witch is! Livvy, Eliza, you must help me defeat her so I can transform . . . like an ugly duckling into a swan. Like a caterpillar into a butterfly. I must be free!'

'Don't worry, Margot.' Olivia stroked the pony's mane to console her. 'We've beaten the witch's magic five times before.'

'But we've never beaten the actual witch face to face,' Eliza pointed out. 'I wonder why she's decided to show herself now?'

'She must be worried that we're close to breaking her spell,' Olivia said.

'Well, of course she is,' Margot sniffled. 'After all, I'm the very last pony in the stables. Once you release me, the spell will be gone for good!'

Olivia and Eliza looked at each other in astonishment.

'Really?' Olivia asked.

'Truly?' Eliza added.

'Really and truly,' Margot replied. 'I'm the last pony, girls. You're almost there. If I'm free, then the witch's dark magic will be unbound and

Spellbound Stables will be ghostly no more!'

'This is amazing!' Olivia said. 'Eliza, isn't it incredible? If we can break the spell on Margot, then all the ponies will be free, the spell will be broken and you'll be a real girl once more.'

'Hmmm, yes, well, some of that is true . . .' Eliza said. 'You see, I've never really explained to you, Livvy, exactly how the spell works. The thing is . . .'

But Olivia was no longer listening. She was too excited.

'We'll break your clumsy curse, Margot. I'm sure that if we practise hard enough, you can learn all the moves and beat that awful Horace and the horrid witch.'

Margot frowned. 'I'm not sure I'm really clumsy—' she began to say but Eliza bounded in over the top of her.

'Ohhh, I have the most genius idea!' Eliza's green eyes

glistened. 'Margot needs a dance teacher – and I know just who we can call on. We must see Madame Fifi!'

'Madame Fifi?' Olivia said. 'Who is she?'

'Only the most famous ballet teacher in all the land!' Eliza said. 'Madame Fifi trains the king's horses in the royal stables to perform their dance moves. I'm sure she could work wonders with Margot.'

'I don't like meeting new people. I'm very, very shy around strangers,' Margot said quietly. But Olivia, who was now extremely animated and talking loudly, didn't hear Margot's protests because she was fizzing with excitement.

'Ah, but Eliza, we do know someone who knows the king – let's ask Prince Patrick!'

'Oh, of course!' Eliza said. 'Prince Patrick owes us a favour. After all, we got him off the hook when he was doomed to marry that awful almost-Princess Petronella.'

Even as the girls hatched their plan, the enchanted mist was already rising up through the straw.

'I hear trumpets,' Olivia said. 'We're on our way to the palace!'

Sure enough, by the time the mist had cleared, the girls and Margot were standing at the gates of the royal palace. The trumpeters were blowing like mad to announce their arrival and a handsome boy on a pure-white horse galloped out to meet them.

'Eliza and Olivia!' Prince Patrick was delighted. 'Have you come to do a spot of swashbuckling? Wait here and I'll go and grab my sword!'

'No, no, Prince Patrick,' Eliza said, 'we're here because we need your help.'

'Of course, of course!' Prince Patrick agreed at once. 'After all, you girls saved me from a terrible fate on my wedding day. How is sweet Sparkle? Does she miss me?'

'She still has your picture on the wall of her stall with a love heart drawn round it,' Olivia said. 'But today it's not Sparkle who needs transforming. Prince Patrick, this is Margot . . . Margot? Now where did she go?'

'Over here,' Margot said meekly. 'I'm hiding behind the royal rose bushes.'

'What on earth are you doing that for?' Eliza said. 'Come on out, Margot, and meet the prince.'

'That's just the thing,' Margot muttered. 'I'm not very good at meeting new people, especially handsome princes.'

'Come on, Margot.' Olivia had to go and lead the pony forth.

'What is this poor pony's curse, then?' Prince Patrick looked kindly upon her.

'Margot is clumsy,' Olivia said confidently.

'I'm really not sure that I am . . .' Margot said even more softly than before.

'Of course she is!' Eliza said brightly. 'She is the sixth Spellbound Pony and if we can lift the curse, then that is all of them done and Spellbound Stables will be free at last.'

'Margot wants to be a dancer, you see,' Olivia continued, 'so we were hoping your Madame Fifi would—'

'Teach her to dance?' Prince Patrick clapped his hands. 'Consider it done! Fifi is the best in the business. As it happens, Fifi is giving a dance lesson to the ponies in the palace right now. I'm sure Margot can join in.'

'Join in?' Margot quivered. 'With the other ponies? Oh, that sounds terrifying!'

But the girls weren't listening – they were too busy following Prince Patrick into the palace

51

and oohing and aahing at all the wonderful sights.

'Your home is very beautiful,' Olivia said with a gasp. 'Look at all the amazing paintings on the walls and the grand collection of priceless, fragile marble statues all along the hallway!'

'It's too grand for me,' Margot whimpered, trotting along nervously beside Olivia. 'Oh, I feel faint and quite overwhelmed with utter shyness.'

The girls didn't seem to hear her.

'I love the way you've precariously placed those extremely delicate crystal goblets on those pedestals,' Eliza pointed out as they breezed further down the hall.

'Yes,' Prince Patrick agreed, 'Mummy – the queen – is quite the collector of very expensive, easy-to-break ornaments!'

'And ohhhh, I hear music up ahead!' Eliza trilled. 'Wonderful, wonderful ballet music!'

'That will be the string quartet,' Prince Patrick said. 'Madame Fifi likes to bring them with her at all times.'

At the door of the dance parlour, Prince Patrick gave the girls and Margot a wink. 'Now, be warned,' he said. 'Madame Fifi has a bit of a gruff manner but her ponies are the best dancers in the land.'

'Gosh,' Margot trembled and bit her lip, 'I *feel sick as a pig. I don't think I can do this! Please, Livvy and Eliza, could you girls go in there without me? Oh nooooo . . .*'

Margot tried to wiggle away but Prince Patrick had already swung open the parlour doors and shoved her into the middle of the room.

Twelve ponies, all of them dressed in
their best ballerina tutus, suddenly stopped
dancing and turned to stare at the newcomer
in their midst.

'Ohhh, eek!' Margot squeaked. 'Everybody *is* staring at me! Ohhh, I'm so shy!'

Prince Patrick looked very hard at the pony trembling in the middle of the parlour.

'Are you girls quite certain that this one is clumsy?' he said. 'Only it seems to me that her problem might actually be—'

'Oh yes,' Olivia and Eliza trilled in unison, 'quite certain. Margot is clumsy.'

'Well,' Prince Patrick said, sighing, 'I suppose this is your sixth Spellbound Pony so you must know what you are doing by now. Come on, then, Margot, buck up! Let me introduce you to Madame Fifi.'

Prince Patrick took hold of the trembling Margot and led her forward to the centre of the room where a very wizened old woman in a pink ballet outfit, holding a candy-striped cane, was inspecting the line of ballerina ponies. She looked at Margot with a critical eye.

'Who is this?' she asked in a snippy tone.

'Madame Fifi,' Prince Patrick said, 'this is Margot – she's a clumsy pony who wants to learn to dance.'

'I really don't think I'm clumsy . . .' Margot muttered, but no one was listening.

'I can teach even the clumsiest pony to be a megastar,' Madame Fifi pronounced. 'Such is the power of Madame Fifi. Now, line up, Margot – there, next to Tinkerbell. Quickly now – we are about to begin our stretches.'

The ponies all scurried to form a line in front of Madame Fifi and began to stretch their legs.

Margot shuffled nervously next to Tinkerbell and gave Olivia a shy look from under her forelock.

Olivia gave Margot a thumbs up and Margot blushed so hard her cheeks turned the colour of Christmas stockings.

'Look at Margot. Oh, she looks so uncomfortably shy out there,' Olivia said. 'Do you know, Eliza, now that I think about it, what with all the hiding away and the blushing and the umming and aahing, well . . . she's quite, shy, isn't she?'

'Is she?' Eliza said. 'She's so quiet most of the time I really don't notice much about her.'

'But isn't that exactly how things are when you are shy?' Olivia mused. 'People really don't notice how you feel because you find it so hard to tell them. In fact, now that I come to think of it, apart from that very first moment when she arrived and crashed into the stall, she hasn't really done anything clumsy at all, has she?'

'She banged into the water trough,' Eliza pointed out.

'No, actually that was me,' Olivia said, 'and my elbow is still a bit ouchy.'

'Oh well, perhaps she is a bit shy, I suppose,' Eliza said. 'Anyway, Livvy, do be quiet now, Madame Fifi is about to begin!'

Chapter Five

Madame Fifi rapped her candy-striped cane hard against the wooden floor of the parlour. 'First positions, please, ponies!'

The ponies all clacked their hooves together and Margot tried to imitate Tinkerbell, who was standing beside her doing stretches.

'Ohhh, Tinkerbell, you are so graceful!' Margot said very quietly. 'I would so love it if we could be *friends*.' Very carefully, Margot reached out, trying to take hold of Tinkerbell's hoof with her own—

'No!' Madame Fifi struck her cane again very hard on the wooden floor. 'No. Holding. Hooves!' she snapped at Margot. 'This is a dance class, not a friendship circle, Margot. Stop that at once!'

The ponies all turned to look at Margot.

'Ohhhh, ohhh, noooo,' Margot whimpered.

'What's going on?' Eliza asked.

'I think,' Olivia said, 'that Margot was trying to make friends with Tinkerbell, which is something that takes a lot of courage when you are very SHY. Except Madame Fifi told her off and now everyone in the room is looking at her and that has made Margot very upset because being the centre of attention is awful when you are SHY!'

Eliza frowned. 'Are you trying to make a point or something, Livvy, because you keep raising your voice whenever you say the word shy!'

'Yes, I am!' Olivia said. 'Eliza, I've just realised – we've got entirely the wrong end of the stick on this one. We thought poor Margot was a clumsy clot but really and truly she's not. I don't think the Pemberley Witch has cursed her to be clumsy at all.

I think Margot was cursed with shyness!'

'Goodness!' Eliza's green eyes went wide. 'Now that you say it, that does make far more sense. All the blushing and whispering and hiding. Of course! Margot is shy.'

'Yes, exactly!' Olivia said. 'And now we've gone and made it worse. Look!'

In the centre of the parlour, Margot was shaking like a leaf as all the ponies stopped to stare at her and Madame Fifi barked instructions.

'Margot!' Madame Fifi snapped. 'I said up on tippy-toes!'

'Eek!' Margot wobbled about. 'I'm trying, Madame Fifi, but it's so hard with everyone watching me. Oh, I do wish you would all stop staring. I wish the ground would swallow me up, in fact!'

'Stop talking, Margot, and go up, up, up on your

toes!' Madame Fifi commanded. 'And . . . now . . . twirl!'

'Twirl?' Margot gulped. 'With everyone looking at me?'

'Yes, twirl!' Madame Fifi demanded. 'Twirl, twirl, twirl!'

'Here I gooooo!' Margot cried.

'She's twirling!' Olivia exclaimed.

'Yes, but where's she going?' Prince Patrick gasped.

'Oh no!' Eliza groaned. 'She's so painfully shy she's only gone and twirled herself right through the door to get away from us all!'

'Uh-oh! She's heading straight for Mummy's priceless collection of marble statues and crystal goblets!' Prince Patrick yelped.

'I'm on it!' Olivia raced after Margot.

'I do hope she makes it in time,' Prince Patrick said.

'I'm sure she will—' Eliza began to say . . . but her words were cut dead by a very loud crash.

'Did that sound like a marble statue breaking into a million tiny pieces to you?' Prince Patrick asked.

'Ummm, possibly,' Eliza said.

There was another loud bang followed by another tinkling crash.

'Did that sound like another statue being dashed

to the floor and shattered beyond repair by a twirling pony?'

'Now that you mention it,' Eliza said, wincing, 'it sounded exactly like that.'

Then a final almighty bang and crash echoed around the room.

'Did that . . .?' Prince Patrick began, but before he could say any more, Olivia and Margot stuck their heads back round the door.

'There's been a bit of an accident in the hallway,' Olivia said carefully. 'Margot would like to apologise but she's a bit too shy to come in here and say sorry herself.'

'She really is shy, isn't she!' Eliza groaned. 'Oh no.'

'She really is,' Olivia agreed. 'Umm, Prince Patrick? You wouldn't happen to have a broom and a dustbin about the place, would you?'

'Never mind that!' Prince Patrick replied. 'If I

were you girls, I would hightail it out of here right now before the queen comes home. Margot will never win the dance contest if Mummy flings you in the dungeons!'

'But you'll get into trouble!' Olivia objected.

'It's all right.' Prince Patrick shrugged. 'I'll tell Mummy I did it in one of my crazy sword fights. I broke her entire Ming vase collection last week and she let me off the hook. Anyway, I owe you girls a favour for getting me out of that dreadful wedding – so now we're even!'

'We most certainly are!' Eliza agreed. 'Thank you, Patrick.'

'Good luck with the dance contest!' Prince Patrick called after them. 'Oh, and Margot? It was lovely to meet you!'

Margot blushed so hard her cheeks started to smoulder a bit with the heat.

'He really is lovely, isn't he?' she whispered
softly as they left the palace. 'No wonder Sparkle
has his posters up all over her bedroom wall. If I
wasn't so painfully shy, I would have asked him
for his autograph.'

'Yes, well, shall we talk about that shyness?'
Olivia sighed. 'Eliza and I both owe you an apology,
Margot. We made a mistake and thought you'd been
cursed to be clumsy but we see now that it was
shyness that was your curse all along.'

'Oh, boo-hoo, it's true!' Margot wept so hard
that her hot cheeks began to produce gusts of steam.
'I'm dreadfully, awfully shy and I would love to
dance and be a star, but I'm too afraid.'

'It's not your fault, Margot,' Eliza said kindly. 'It's
the curse – and now that we've figured it out at last,
we're going to find a way to set you free.'

'Absolutely!' Livvy agreed.

'We haven't given up on you,' Eliza insisted.
'We're going to unbind you. Aren't we, Livvy?'

'Absolutely!' Livvy confirmed.

'Oh, thank you, girls! That means the world
to me.' Margot swished her tail with joy, and as she

did so there was an ominous sound of a stone bust falling and cracking on the ground.

'Gosh, I actually was clumsy that time,' Margot blushed.

'Never mind!' Eliza said. 'Margot, perhaps we should get out of here?'

'Absolutely Triple-Absolutely!' Livvy agreed. 'This new curse is going to prove hard to beat and if we're going to win the dance contest, we'll need a cunning plan.'

Chapter Six

Back at Pemberley Stables, Olivia tucked Margot up in her stall.

'Poor pony, what a rough day.' Olivia shut the stall door behind her softly. 'Let's be quiet and let her nap.'

'What are we going to do?' Eliza sighed as they sat down together on the hay bales outside. 'The dance competition is looming, and—'

'Hang on!' Olivia said. 'What's that noise?'

'How strange . . . it's like the pounding of drums and it seems to be coming from inside Margot's stall!' Eliza said.

'Yikes,' Olivia exclaimed. 'I can feel the floor shaking! Oh no. What's happening? I'm almost too scared to look.'

Olivia swung the door to the stall open wide and gasped in shock. 'Margot? What on earth?'

Margot was on the ceiling of her stall, clinging with all four legs to the rather creaky-looking old metal chandelier.

'Oh my goodness,' Olivia squeaked, 'how in heaven's name did she end up there?'

'What's more, how are we going to get her down?' Eliza added.

At that moment the thumping drums started up again, and with a wild swing from the chandelier, Margot leapt into thin air and flew away from them.

71

With a graceful swish of her tail, she landed in the middle of the stable . . . and then, as the drums began to thump harder, Margot started to sing.

'Whump, whump, whump, shakin' my rump, rump, rump!' she trilled. 'I like to move, move, move, and I love to groove, groove, groove . . .'

'Are you seeing this?' Olivia asked. 'She's amazing!'

'Utterly!' Eliza whispered. 'She's wild – the most fun dancer I've ever seen in my life!'

'Do you think she's noticed that we're here?' Olivia whispered.

'No,' Eliza replied, 'I don't think she's seen us yet.'

'Whooo-whooo!' Margot was bouncing about her stall now, wiggling her hips and shaking her mane. 'Wiggle it, jiggle it, like a pig-a-let!' And with a tremendous flying spin, she turned and came face to face with the girls.

'Eek!' Margot leaped behind the door to hide. 'Livvy and Eliza – I had no idea you were there. Oh, how embarrassing!'

'Margot,' Olivia helped her up, 'that was flat-out amazing! I never knew you could dance like that.'

'Really?' Margot came out from behind the door, eyes wide with surprise. 'You mean you like my bonkers dancing?'

'Why didn't you show us your moves before?' Olivia asked.

'Well, that's the thing,' Margot said with a sigh. 'I'm too shy . . .'

'Do you think you could dance like that in the contest?' Olivia asked.

'Oh, I don't think so, Livvy.' Margot shook her mane. 'It's the crowds, you see – what with the judges and all those people watching. I feel sick at the thought of it and when that happens,

I begin to panic and my pulse gets very quick and my tummy feels queasy . . . and the next thing you know I have four left feet.'

'But you were so graceful just now,' Eliza said.

'Yes, but there was no one here to watch me, was there?' Margot sighed again. 'I didn't see you girls come in. That's the problem. I'm fine dancing on my own here in my own stall, but the minute I'm stuck in front of an audience, I can feel the sweat on my hooves and my mind goes blank and then I get my fetlocks in a twist.'

'Hmmm . . .' Olivia pondered this. 'Well, this is a pickle. With the competition almost upon us, we've only just discovered that our very last Spellbound Pony is suffering from a case of terrible shyness and now we need her to overcome it in order to win a dance contest in front of hundreds of people.'

'Oh, my goodness.' Margot wobbled about like she was going to faint. 'Hundreds of people? Oh nooooo . . .'

'Stay calm, Margot.' Eliza said. 'Livvy and I will find a way to break the spell. After all, that's what we do, isn't it, Livvy?'

Olivia looked very worried. 'Yes, of course, Margot. You get a good night's sleep and we'll think of a plan by morning, in time for the contest.'

But as Olivia left the stables and headed for home that evening, she had a sinking feeling. Would the very last pony in Spellbound Stables prove to be the one that was impossible to save?

There were yummy smells when Olivia arrived home and music was blaring all through the house. She found her mother in the kitchen, dancing and bopping about in time to the stereo as she put the pasta on to boil.

'What's for dinner, Mum?'

'Oh, hi, Livvy.' Mrs Campbell turned from the stove and danced over to her daughter. 'It's spaghetti bolognaise. You're just in time. I could do with some help setting the table.'

Olivia grabbed the plates from the cupboard and found herself watching her mother as she boogied about. 'You're a very good dancer, Mum.'

'Well, I should be!' Mrs Campbell giggled. 'Remember, your mum was a professional ballerina back in the day. Before you and Ella were born, I danced my way through the whole of Europe with my tutus and my pointe slippers.'

'Do you have photos,' Olivia asked, 'from when you were a ballerina?'

'Of course I do.' Mrs Campbell went over to the

sideboard and pulled out an album. She flicked open the page to a picture of a beautiful ballerina in a sparkly tutu wearing a golden mask that hid her face.

'That's me!' Mrs Campbell laughed. 'It's amazing the difference a costume makes – it's like being a different person.'

'Oh my goodness, that's it!' Olivia squeaked. She threw her arms round her mother. 'Oh, Mum, thanks – you've solved everything as always!'

'Have I?' Mrs Campbell frowned. 'Well, I'm not sure what you mean, but that's lovely of you to say so, Livvy.'

'Mum,' Olivia said, 'do you still have all your old ballet costumes?'

'Yes, as it happens,' Mrs Campbell said. 'They're in a big trunk in the attic. Why?'

'I need to borrow them,' Olivia said. 'I have a friend with a very important dance contest tomorrow, and I think I just figured out a way to help her win!'

Chapter Seven

When Olivia arrived back at the stables the next day she found Eliza trying desperately to coax the Spellbound Pony out of her stall.

'Margot is so shy today she won't even speak to me,' Eliza sighed.

'Margot?' Olivia knocked on the stall door. 'It's me. Livvy. Can Eliza and I come in?'

'I don't know.' The pony's voice quivered. She

sounded weepy. 'I want to let you in, but . . .
ohhh, I'm feeling very, very shy.'

'It's all right,' Olivia said gently. 'We're your
friends, remember?'

'That's true.' Margot sniffled. 'You are my
friends. Okay, Livvy, you can both come in.'

Olivia and Eliza entered the stall and found
the pony sitting in the corner looking thoroughly
miserable.

'Ohhh, Livvy,' Margot said with another sniff,
'I'm so sorry to let you girls down. I know that
all the ponies in the stables are depending on
me to win the competition today. But Livvy and
Eliza, I just can't do it – I'm too shy! There's no
way I can go out there and dance in front of the
judges and everyone.'

'I know, I know, Margot,' Olivia said kindly. 'It
must be awful feeling so painfully shy. But what if I

told you that you didn't have to be the one out there doing the dancing? What if I said that another pony was going to dance instead of you?'

Margot suddenly stopped sniffling. 'So I wouldn't have to dance at all? It would be another pony entirely?'

'Well, not entirely . . . but sort of,' Olivia said.

'Whatever do you mean, Livvy?' Eliza was baffled. 'It has to be Margot who wins the dancing contest – that's the only way we can break the spell.'

'It will be Margot . . . but it also won't be,' Olivia said.

'Well, now you're making even less sense than you did before!' Eliza rolled her eyes. 'And what is that gigantic sack you've brought with you, by the way?'

Olivia patted the bulging sack she had dragged all the way to the stables. 'This sack contains everything we need to help Margot win,' Olivia explained. 'Oh – and I threw in a dress for you to change into, Eliza.

Now, both of you must trust me because we're running out of time. The mist is beginning to rise and we need to leave now if we're going to make it in time for the contest. So what do you say? Are we a team?'

Olivia put her hand out.

'Two brave girls together!' Eliza put her misty, ghostly hand on top of Olivia's and then both of them looked at Margot, who blushed and trembled.

'Come on! Be brave, Margot; we will help you overcome your shyness, I swear!' Olivia said.

'Oh, okay.' Margot offered her hoof. 'I'm in. Let's win.'

'Two brave girls and one Spellbound Pony!' Olivia cried. 'Hooray – let's dance!' The mist rose and filled the stable as Eliza, Olivia and Margot stood united, and when at last it had cleared, they were no longer in Margot's stall. They were in a green room.

'Oh, wow!' Olivia looked at the golden star on the door. 'Margot, this is your dressing room! This is where you'll get ready before you dance.'

'But, Livvy!' Margot looked very worried. 'I thought you said I didn't have to dance at all, that another pony would take my place?'

'Exactly!' Olivia said. She began to pull out the contents of the sack. 'That other pony, Margot, is going to be you!'

In the grand ballroom at Pemberley Manor the dance contest was already under way.

'And what a marvellous display we've had here today!' the commentator trilled over the sound system. 'So many wonderful dancers. And now it's time for the favourite combination of the competition. These two are bound to win – or at least, that's what they told me. They're very confident! So without further ado let us welcome to the dance floor the almost-already-winners . . . Horace the Hunt Master and the Pemberley Witch!'

Into the spotlight strutted Horace, dressed in a very puffy tutu.

'Gosh, look at his head wobbling in time with the music,' Eliza whispered.

'He's got rhythm, I'll give him that,' Olivia agreed.

'Look – here comes the witch!'

The Pemberley Witch joined her dance partner under the spotlight and together, as the crowd went silent, they struck a dramatic pose, the witch gripping a rose between her teeth as Horace held her in his arms.

'It's going to be a tango!' the announcer called out. 'What a crowd-pleaser! Off they go . . .'

'Uh-oh,' Olivia said. 'Look at them swanning about cheek to cheek. They look unbeatable!'

'I wouldn't speak too soon,' Eliza remarked. 'They seem to be squabbling.'

It was true. On the dance floor, Horace and the witch were arguing.

'It's my turn to lead, Pembers,' Horace grumped. 'You promised me!'

'Never mind that!' the witch snapped. 'I've been biting on this rose and now I've got a thorn stuck in my lip—'

'Dip?' Horace said. 'Did you say you want me to dip?'

'No, I said lip!' the witch shrieked. But it was too late. Horace had flung her back towards the floor in an exotic dance move.

'The witch is down,' Olivia gasped.

'Oh, but she's made it look like it was all part of the dance!' Eliza said.

Sprawled on the floor, the witch was now kicking her legs up high in the air.

'She's lost one of her ruby glitter shoes,' Olivia observed.

But even losing her footwear failed to sway the judges, and when the dance was over and they held up their cards, all three of them had given Horace and the Pemberley Witch perfect marks!

'Three tens!' Eliza squeaked. 'Who would have thought?'

'Yes.' Olivia narrowed her eyes. 'It's almost as if they were enchanted, don't you think, Eliza?'

'Oh yes, of course!' Eliza said. 'The witch has cast a spell on the judges! How can Margot possibly beat a score like that?'

'We're about to find out,' Olivia commented.

'The next contestant is our final competitor of the night,' the announcer said. 'I don't have a name here, so I can't tell you who it is. All it says is: FINAL COMPETITOR OF THE NIGHT. . .'

Silence descended upon the ballroom. Not a sound could be heard. Then, in the darkness, the spotlight flooded the dance floor, and there, caught in its brilliant beam, was a pony. She was a beautiful dapple-grey in a tutu that was every colour of the rainbow, smothered in sparkling gemstones, and on her face she wore a rainbow-coloured, diamond-studded mask!

'Ladies and gentlemen,' the announcer said, 'let's hear it for the Masked Dancer!'

Disguised by her sparkly mask, Margot took a deep bow and then, as the music set a thumping beat, she began to dance.

'Oh my.' Eliza was stunned. 'She is amazing! What did Margot call that move, anyway?'

'She's doing the flamingo!' Olivia clapped with delight as masked-Margot pecked her way around the dance floor on one leg.

'Oh, and that move is the playing possum!' Eliza cheered as Margot swooshed about on her back.

'The mouse in a rucksack!' Olivia was pumping her hands in the air. 'Oh, the crowd loves it – they're going bonkers!'

'Look,' Eliza said, 'the judges love it too! They've all voted with their boards and every single one of them has given the Masked Dancer a ten! Oh, Livvy, do you know what this means? It's a tie!'

'In your face, Horace!' Olivia whooped for joy. 'Margot has done it – there's going to be a dance-off!'

Chapter Eight

Backstage in her dressing room, still wearing her sparkly mask and rainbow tutu, Margot was bouncing around with such great excitement she could barely keep her hooves on the ground.

'Ohhh, ohhh, ohhh, girls!' she squeaked as she bounded about like a rainbow-glitter ping-pong ball. 'Did you see me out there?'

'We certainly did,' Eliza said. 'The judges gave

the Masked Dancer a perfect score!'

'Yes – what a genius idea it was to wear a mask, Livvy,' Margot said. 'Nobody knew it was me so I didn't feel shy at all!'

'You didn't look shy – in fact, you were amazing!' Olivia agreed.

'Unfortunately, Horace and the witch got a perfect score too,' Eliza pointed out, 'so now you will need to beat them in the dance-off.'

'Back out there again?' Margot whimpered. 'In front of all those people?'

'Don't think about the audience,' Olivia told her. 'Dance as if there's nobody watching.'

Margot took a deep breath, 'Okay, Livvy, good advice.'

'Ohhh, I hear the music starting up now,' Eliza said, 'which means Horace and the witch are about to go back on. Quick, Livvy! Let's watch from the grandstand.'

As the girls ran to take their seats in time, Olivia felt a pang of worry. 'I hope Margot will be okay,' she said. 'Performing in front of such a huge crowd is scary for a very shy pony.'

'It is very crowded,' Eliza agreed, 'but look up there. Two empty seats!'

'Girls!' It was Prince Patrick waving to them from the grandstand. 'I've saved you seats.' He gestured to the unoccupied spaces beside him. 'Come and sit with me and Madame Fifi.'

Olivia and Eliza squished their way through the crowds and flung themselves down in their seats just as the lights dimmed and a spotlight struck the dance floor . . . which was totally empty!

'Where are Horace and the witch?' Olivia wondered aloud.

Suddenly, the spotlight swerved wildly to alight upon a witch's hat lying in the middle of the dance floor.

'Why is there a hat on the floor?' Eliza asked.

'Wait a minute, is it moving?' Olivia gasped.

The hat scooted about as if it had a life of its own and then suddenly, from beneath the brim, two legs appeared and began to dance.

'Hold on . . .' Olivia glared at the dancing legs. 'I know those glittery red shoes!'

There was a wild cackle from beneath the hat and a moment later the witch popped out and began to dance a frantic jig. Then she kicked both legs over her head and dropped into the splits.

'That witch is really very nimble for a little old lady,' Olivia had to admit as she observed the witch go into a backflip and begin to caterpillar her way across the dance floor.

'She's the talented one in the combo. She's absolutely carrying Horace,' Eliza agreed.

'Actually –' Prince Patrick pointed to the contestants – 'the witch really is carrying Horace – look!'

Out on the dance floor Horace had made his entrance by leaping into the air and the witch had caught him above her head as lightly as if he were a cloud, and was now spinning him in circles.

'Ohhh, that is a good move,' Olivia had to admit, 'and the judges are loving it.'

'The witch certainly has them under her spell,' Patrick agreed.

'Exactly!' Olivia said. 'She really does have them under a spell. The judges are enchanted! That's how the witch and Horace got their perfect score last time. It will take a real upset to break her fiendish magic.'

'Oh, what are they doing now?' Eliza wondered as Horace and the witch pressed up cheek to cheek and strutted to the centre of the dance floor.

'Why, they're going into the dance medley.' The announcer answered her question. 'First up, it's the rumba!'

'Rumba, rumba under there – who wants to see my underwear!' the witch hooted as she flicked up her skirts.

'Tens all round from the judges!' the announcer trilled. 'And now the boogie-woogie!'

'Ewww,' Olivia said, 'I think the witch just picked her nose!'

'Bogey-wogey!' the witch cackled.

Eliza sighed. 'It doesn't seem to matter how awful she is, the judges are in her thrall. They just gave them another perfect round of tens.'

'At this point, they are unbeatable,' Olivia groaned.

'Now ... for the grand finale ...' There was a drum roll as the announcer spoke. 'They've chosen the foxtrot!'

The music changed and Horace and the witch struck a pose, ready to strut their stuff, except ...

'What is that noise?' Olivia asked.

'It sounds like hounds baying,' Eliza said.

'And horses galloping,' added Prince Patrick.

At that moment, a ginger creature with a very bushy tail and bright eyes shot through the ballroom at a pace.

'Why, it's a fox,' Eliza said. 'Look – here comes the hunt chasing after him!'

Through the ballroom there now scampered a pack of drooling, unruly hounds, all running hard

on the scent of the fox, and behind them, riders on horseback cantered boldly, leaping this way and that.

'Horace has brought an entire fox hunt with him to foxtrot!' Olivia groaned.

'Look,' Eliza said, 'the judges don't like it! The chaos has broken the spell a bit and they've given him sixes and sevens!'

'That means Margot is still in it to win it!' Prince Patrick sat on the edge of his seat. 'Come on, Margot!'

Horace and the witch exited the dance floor looking puffed and pink in the cheeks, and now the spotlight flitted about once more, looking for the next contestant.

'Here she comes,' the announcer said. 'The Masked Dancer!'

There was silence. The spotlight stayed empty.

Olivia felt panic rising in her. 'Where is she?'

'Perhaps she was overcome by shyness at the last minute.' Eliza bit her lip. 'Oh no. Come on, Margot!'

'Yes, come on, Margot!' Madame Fifi called out.

Soon the entire crowd was chanting: 'Margot! Margot! Margot!'

'This might only make matters worse, you know,' Olivia said. 'Margot is already shy. Hearing everyone call her name may just drive her away completely—'

'Look!' Eliza squeaked. 'There she is!'

In the spotlight stood a dapple-grey pony in a silver ballet tutu.

'The Masked Dancer at last!' the announcer said. 'Are you ready to begin?'

In the spotlight, the Masked Dancer shook her head.

'Why doesn't she dance? What is she doing?' a member of the audience shouted out.

'I'm doing something I should have done from the very start,' Margot replied. Then she took off the mask and the crowd gasped.

'I'm going to dance as if no one is watching.'

Chapter Nine

Margot had taken off the mask ... but she wasn't dancing.

'Oh no,' Eliza gasped. 'She's so overwhelmed with shyness that she can't move!'

'Ohhhh no!' Olivia squeaked. 'I had hoped that showing her she could dance with the mask on would overcome her shyness. But look at her – she's frozen on the spot. Poor Margot!'

Then suddenly, the music started – a jazzy drum beat with a catchy tune.

'Look,' Olivia said, 'Margot's tail! It's twitching!'

'And her hoof,' Eliza pointed out. 'It's beginning to tap along.'

Under the brilliant glare of the spotlight, Margot raised her muzzle to the sky, struck a dramatic pose and gave Olivia and Eliza a sneaky wink.

'Aha . . . Margot's not feeling shy!' Olivia laughed. 'This is all part of the dance. She's putting on a show!'

At that moment, Margot's hoof-taps became quick and frantic like the beat of the drums, her metal horseshoes clacking more and more loudly. Then the tempo changed, and in one graceful leap and a swish of her rump, Margot began to rumba.

'The crowd are going wild!' Eliza cried. 'Listen to that applause. They love her!'

'Of course they do.' Madame Fifi clapped her

hands in delight. 'She has great moves!'

Sweeping across the floor now, Margot broke into a tango.

'I thought it took two to tango,' Madame Fifi said, 'but Margot is so amazing she can even tango solo! What a star she is. In all my years as a dance teacher I've never seen anything like it. The judges will surely give her perfect marks for this routine!'

'Look at her twirls,' Eliza said. 'Margot is spinning so fast, I can hardly see her! She's become a complete blur.'

'Oh no.' Prince Patrick leaped from his seat. 'The poor pony. Look, she's fallen down – she must be dizzy from all that spinning!'

'Calm yourself, Your Royal Highness,' Madame Fifi said. 'Margot didn't fall down. Why, it's obvious that she's doing the world's most famous ballet move

– the dying swan! It's the grand finale from Swan Lake!'

It was true. Margot was spreadeagled on the floor and flapping her fetlocks as if her legs were wings.

'The crowd are throwing roses at her,' Olivia cried. 'Bravo, Margot!'

With tears of joy in her eyes, Margot looked up at the grandstands filled with thousands of people and swished her tail with delight, rising to take a bow and blowing kisses to the crowd.

'She's thriving on all this attention,' Olivia laughed. 'She's not the least bit shy any more!'

'What a star!' Prince Patrick agreed. 'In fact, speaking of stars, is it just me or has Margot suddenly become extra shiny? What is that golden light glowing from her?'

'It's the spell!' Olivia cried. 'Margot is transforming – she's a real horse again!'

'It looks like the witch's enchantment over the judges has been broken too,' Eliza squealed. 'All three of them have raised their scorecards and given Margot tens. She's won the dance-off!'

Lady Luella stepped into the spotlight with a golden trophy in her hands. 'This is for you, Margot,' she said. 'Congratulations—'

'Hey, pony, get your thieving hooves off my trophy!'

Suddenly a bat-like creature swooped into view and made a grab for the golden prize. 'The trophy must be mine!' the Pemberley Witch shouted as she tried to yank it clean out of Lady Luella's hands. 'Give it to me!'

'I don't think so!' Lady Luella snatched it straight back. 'Margot won that trophy fair and square – which is more than I can say for you and Horace, with your magical enchantments!'

'I want that trophy!' The witch stomped up and down, banging her feet against the wooden floor like an elephant.

'Is that a new dance,' Olivia called out, 'or just a temper tantrum?'

The whole crowd laughed at this, which only made the witch even more furious.

'You're all going to pay for mocking me!' the Pemberley Witch fumed as she stamped and stomped on the floor even more noisily. 'You're all going to payyyyyy—'

'Gosh,' Prince Patrick remarked, 'look at that. She's stomped all the way through the floorboards!'

Olivia, Eliza and the prince raced down to look at the hole in the floor.

'It looks as if it goes all the way to Outer Mongolia,' Prince Patrick said.

'Then I don't imagine we'll be seeing her again for a while,' Lady Luella said. 'Good show. She proved to be a nasty piece of knitting in the end.'

'Well, I'm very glad she's gone . . . and all of the Spellbound Ponies have been set free!' Olivia patted Margot on her glossy dapple-grey neck. 'Isn't it amazing, Eliza? We've done it! We've unbound them all and now Pemberley Stables will be restored to its former glory.'

Olivia had expected her best friend to be every bit as overjoyed as she was, but when she looked at

Eliza standing beside her in the spotlight, she saw that she was crying.

'Eliza?' Olivia was confused. 'Why are you crying? This is good news! We've broken the witch's curse. The ponies have been saved, and now that they're all free, there's no need for you to be trapped by the witch's curse, either. You can become a real girl at last and we can really be best friends!'

'Oh, Livvy,' Eliza said, 'if only that were true.'

A haunting, ghostly chuckle rang through the ballroom at that moment and Horace stepped into the spotlight.

'Really? Silly Olivia! Did you think all this time when you were saving the ponies that one day you would save Eliza too? Clearly you don't understand the true nature of the witch's spell.'

Olivia's heart was pounding as she turned to her best friend.

113

'Eliza?' Olivia said. 'What does he mean? Surely now the spell is broken you're going to transform just like the ponies? Eliza? Tell me you will!'

'Oh, Livvy!' Eliza was weeping now, and her glistening tears shone like liquid stardust against her alabaster skin. 'I've been trying to explain to you for so long but I could never find the words. The ponies are different from me, you see. I'm a ghost, and I always will be.'

'Poor Olivia.' Lady Luella stepped into the spotlight. 'Now do you see the truth? The ponies are all free and the curse is broken. There is nothing to bind my daughter to Spellbound Stables any more.'

Lady Luella wiped the ghostly tears from Eliza's cheeks, cupped her daughter's chin in her hand and smiled. 'Dear heart,' she said, 'it's time for you to come home.'

Chapter Ten

Olivia felt as if her heart was breaking into a million pieces. 'So you'll never be a nine-year-old girl again?' Tears brimmed in her eyes and her voice was shaking. 'But, Eliza, we had all those wonderful plans for Pemberley Stables. There was so much we were going to do together!'

'I never had the heart to tell you,' Eliza said, 'but you must have known deep down, Olivia, that once all the ponies were free and the spell was broken, I would have to go.'

Olivia choked back her tears. 'It's true. I guess I always knew,' she whispered, 'but I don't want you to leave me, Eliza. You are my best friend.'

'Oh, Livvy!' Eliza said. 'You are my best friend too. In two hundred and nine years I never dreamed I could ever meet someone as amazing, loyal and brave as you.'

'Does it really have to be goodbye, though?' Olivia sniffled. 'Can't you come back to Pemberley Stables with me and haunt the place just a little longer?'

'It's how magic works, I'm afraid.' Eliza sighed. 'The spell is broken – I can feel the enchantment lifting and I know that I cannot return.'

'Then I'll stay here with you!' Olivia said firmly. 'I can live in Pemberley Manor and make ghost pavlova and have duck races and—'

'Livvy, I would love that,' Eliza said, 'but you can't stay with me. The ponies need you now more than ever.'

As if to confirm this, Margot gave a snort and stamped on the floor. Now that she was a real pony and no longer spellbound, she couldn't talk any more, but she was making her feelings quite clear.

'All this time, Livvy, I've been teaching you to take over from me,' Eliza said. 'You know how to care for the ponies, how to groom, feed and rug them up nice and warm in winter. You're ready now. They'll be in good hands. You can run your own riding stables and take care of all of the ponies and give them hugs and make sure they are loved. Because you love ponies as much as I do – I think that's why you were able to open the stable door that very first day. Do you remember how the door magically flew open at your touch? So you see you must go back to Pemberley Stables. And I . . . I must stay here. Mama has missed me terribly for so long and the manor is my home.'

'Will I never, ever see you again?' Olivia asked, the tears welling in her eyes once more.

'Oh, I wouldn't say that!' Eliza smiled. 'Pemberley Stables are very magical, as you know, and things are always afoot. So perhaps one day we will meet again.'

Eliza looked down at the dress that she had borrowed from Olivia.

'Would you mind if I kept the clothes you lent me?' she asked. 'Only I've grown very attached to dressing like a modern girl, and it will be something to remind me of you.'

'Of course I don't mind,' Olivia said, 'and I know in my heart too, Eliza, that we will meet again. A friendship as powerful and true as this one can never be taken away.'

Even as she was saying the words, though, Olivia could sense the enchanted mist rising up around her ankles. She took hold of Margot's mane to keep the pony close to her and clung on tightly as the mist consumed them.

'Goodbye, Eliza,' she whispered, 'until next time.'

On the wall of Spellbound Stables, there was once a poem written in the stone.

The deepest magic binds these stables
Unless two brave girls can turn the tables.
The curse on each horse must be found,
Then break their spell to be unbound.

Those words are gone now and so is Eliza, the ghost who lived there for two hundred years and looked after the Spellbound Ponies. It would be tempting to believe then, that the adventures of Olivia and Eliza were over. But for all we know, they were only just about to begin . . .

START YOUR SPELLBOUND PONIES
ADVENTURE RIGHT AT THE BEGINNING
WITH BOOK ONE . . .

Out Now

CAN THEY SAVE THEM ALL?

Spellbound Ponies
Wishes and Weddings

STACY GREGG

Out Now

CAN THEY SAVE THEM ALL?

Spellbound Ponies
Sugar and Spice

STACY GREGG

Out Now

CAN THEY SAVE THEM ALL?

Spellbound Ponies
Magic and Mischief

STACY GREGG

Collect

Out Now

Out Now

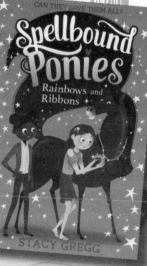

Out Now

them all!